Ellen Gor

Weekly Reader Children's Book Club presents

Kalu and the Wild Boar

KALU and the

1973 New York

WILD BOAR

by Peter Hallard

FRANKLIN WATTS, INC.

Library of Congress Cataloging in Publication Data

Kalu and the wild boar.

SUMMARY: A thirteen-year-old boy of India
tangles courageously with a tiger and a wild boar to
save his father's crops.
[1. Children in India—Fiction. 2. India—
Fiction] I. Mars, Witold T., illus. II. Title.
PZ7.C269Kal   [Fic]   72-8916
ISBN 0-531-02600-0

Design by Diana Hrisinko

Weekly Reader Children's Book Club Edition

Contents

Kalu and the Wild Boar

Battle at dawn

As *the gray light on the eastern hills brightened,*
Kalu's fears increased. The thieves who had been
busy in the field throughout the night would leave
before the sun rose, and Kalu's father, Kunwar Lal,
was guarding the gap in the thorn hedge through
which they would have to make their retreat.
Kunwar Lal was not the man to let them get away
unpunished.

Throughout the night thirteen-year-old Kalu
had been perched on a flimsy bamboo platform
some six feet above the ground. Like his father he
was armed with a metal tin and a rusty iron spike.
By banging on the rusty tin, he and his father had
hoped to frighten away the family of wild pigs
that had been coming to their field or the past
week, eating and trampling down the growing
crop.

No matter how they banged their gongs, the four-legged thieves had not been scared away. Nor could Kalu do more than make them grunt when he fired sun-baked balls of clay at the pigs with his sling. For the first few hours of the night there had been a moon, and it was possible to see the pigs wandering about, eating the grain and trampling lanes in the growing crop.

Kalu's father had brought along a spear, and if he had thought he had a chance, he would certainly have tried to kill the leader of the wild pigs, for their devastation of his crop threatened to ruin him. It was the thought of his father tackling the boar that made the boy shiver with fear. The people of the Indian village of Chandwari had already named the boar *Burra Dhantwallah* (the big-tusked one), and it was a name he well deserved.

Once during the night the boar had come quite close to the platform on which Kalu crouched, and he had seen the tusks glinting in the moonlight. They were long and curved upward from the lower jaw—terrible weapons in a fight.

As the light grew brighter, the boar began to grunt, and at once all the pigs moved toward him. Seconds later Burra Dhantwallah came in sight. He walked into an open space where the grain had all been eaten and the stalks trodden flat. It provided a clear area in which the family could gather together, and was less than thirty feet from the platform on which young Kalu crouched.

Looking up the field toward his father, Kalu saw two arms making a motion. His father was calling on him to use his sling. Dry-lipped and frightened though he was, Kalu grabbed several of the sun-baked clay balls. They were about an inch in diameter, and at such a short range they could hurt.

"I'll aim for his head," Kalu muttered. "If I could blind him in one eye, then he might not come here again."

As the rest of the wild pigs began to merge with their leader, Kalu knelt, took careful aim, and sent a shot singing through the cool morning air. There was an angry grunt almost at once. Kalu had not managed to hit Burra Dhantwallah in a vital spot, but he had struck him just below the left eye.

At the grunt the rest of the pigs quickened their pace while Kalu hurriedly fired a second shot. Burra Dhantwallah had his mouth partly open, and the hard clay ball went straight into the boar's throat. For a moment Burra Dhantwallah stood as if paralyzed. Then he reared on his short but powerful hind legs. He gave a tearing, coughing grunt, and a moment later he had gotten rid of the clay ball.

Kalu was already firing his third shot, and again his aim was good. This time he struck the boar hard on the ear, bringing another angry grunt of pain. It was as Kalu was about to fire his fourth shot that Burra Dhantwallah realized where the stinging shots were coming from. Kalu's movements made the rickety platform sway a little. The bamboo creaked, and the boar heard the sound.

Kalu never fired his fourth shot. He had to grab at the side of the platform to avoid over-balancing, and in the next few seconds Burra Dhantwallah was charging.

Standing a yard high at the shoulder and a good five feet from snout to the tip of his little tail, the boar weighed several hundred pounds. Nor was there any fat on him. He was all bone, muscle, and sinew. He did not charge the platform, or he would have brought it crashing to the ground at once. Instead, he reared on his hind legs and tried to slash at Kalu with his vicious-looking tusks.

The platform swayed horribly, forcing a scream of terror from Kalu. Thinly across the field came a yell from Kunwar Lal: "Bang your plate, my son, bang your plate!" And Kunwar Lal began to bang his metal plate and shout as loudly as he could.

Burra Dhantwallah's family panicked. They turned up the gentle slope and headed for the hilltop. But their lord and master was made of sterner stuff than any of them. If he had an enemy, he preferred to fight him at once. This gave his family a better chance of getting out of danger.

On his four legs again, he slashed angrily at one of the bamboo supports of Kalu's platform. Kalu wailed again as the platform shivered under the blow.

"Bang your plate, bang your plate!" his father bellowed, and continued banging his plate in an effort to distract the boar. Burra Dhantwallah was not listening. He drew back to get a good look at the platform with the young Indian crouched on top. Then he charged.

His snout was hardened by years of rooting in sun-baked soil, and though it must have given him some pain when he struck one of the platform supports with his snout, it did what he wanted. The bamboo snapped with a brittle cracking sound, and the platform tilted. Burra Dhantwallah charged again, and the platform collapsed just as Kalu leaped clear. He dropped to his knees, took one terrified glance behind him, then ran.

For all his ponderous size the boar was amazingly nimble. He spun around on his back feet, gave an angry grunt, then rushed after the boy. Up the slope Kalu's father was shrieking commands: "This way, Kalu . . . come to me, come to me!" And at the same time he was leaping off his platform, though his only weapon was a six-foot bamboo tipped with a spearhead.

The growing grain was over a yard high, and though it had been trampled badly in places by the feeding pigs, there were other places where it was thick. Kalu seemed to be forcing his way through a jungle, and all the time he could hear the angry grunting of Burra Dhantwallah and the stamping of his small hoofs on the hard ground.

He knew his father was racing toward him, yelling encouragement; but he also had a sick feeling that before he would cover the fifty yards that now separated them, the boar would catch up with him.

Suddenly he ran out of the tall grain into a space eaten clear of all but low stubble. Now he could hear the snorting of Burra Dhantwallah.

Then came a scream from his father: "Turn left
. . . turn left . . . leave him to me!"

Kalu turned left, leaping to safety as the boar
was almost at his heels. He looked toward his father
and stopped dead. Kunwar Lal was not a big man.
Years of terribly hard work and poor feeding had
kept him small and lean. Now he stood and faced
the charging boar who must have weighed five
times as much as his human opponent.

In the growing light—for the sun had now
tipped the hills—Kalu saw his father draw back his
right arm. He saw the spear held steady for a moment; then the yellow bamboo shaft hurled through
the air—and missed!

A trap for a wild boar

Even in that moment of terrible danger, Kunwar Lal was thinking of his son. As he turned and began to run, he shouted to Kalu to run for the village. It was a command Kalu could not obey. His legs seemed to have turned to jelly, and his knees were shaking.

He watched Burra Dhantwallah throw up a little cloud of yellow dust as he dug his hoofs into the ground. He saw the big boar turn to chase Kunwar Lal, then spin round and race for the gap in the thorn hedge. He followed the rest of his family and was soon lost to sight in the bushes which dotted the hillside.

About a minute passed before Kalu was joined by his father. Kunwar Lal had been so sure that the boar would follow him that he did not stop until he had reached the one small tree growing in his field, and hurled himself into its lower branches.

When he returned and picked up his spear, he wiped the beads of sweat from his forehead with one hand while he stared incredulously at the spearhead. There was blood on it.

"I must have grazed him," he muttered. "Yet the spear seemed to go right over his head. Perhaps I nicked an ear."

Kalu was still shaking from fright and could only nod agreement when his father said: "We won't say anything about this to anyone, my son. If your mother knew what a fright we have had, she would be terrified. We will just say that I drew blood. Maybe Burra Dhantwallah will have learned a lesson and will not come to our field again. If he does," he added sadly, "then we shall go hungry during the winter. Already they have flattened more than a quarter of our crop."

The following morning when they went to begin the endless weeding, they saw that the thorn hedge which they had closed up so carefully the previous afternoon had once more been ripped apart. "We will help you to build the hedge even stronger," the village headman promised. "Surely

Burra Dhantwallah will tire of breaking it down night after night."

"By the time he tires, I shall be without a crop," Kunwar Lal said grimly. "No, Headman, I must do something. I want you to call a meeting of the Village Council tonight to listen to a plan. I am going to kill Burra Dhantwallah."

There were grunts of disapproval from the other men and shaking of heads. Kalu wondered what his father meant to do, and that night when the men met outside the *bania's* (shopkeeper's) little house, he crouched in the darkness to listen.

"I don't know what the plan of Kunwar Lal is for trying to kill the big boar," the village headman began, "but I am hoping that before long the tiger which we have heard calling in the hills for the past three nights will come down and do the job for us."

"I cannot wait for the tiger," Kunwar Lal said coldly. "The pigs are eating my crops. If they were eating your crops, you would maybe think as I do that the boar should be killed."

"It is bad luck that your field is the end one, and the pigs chose it," one of the older men suggested.

"But when they have eaten all my crop, they will start on the next field, and then the one after that," Kunwar Lal pointed out. "If we do not kill the boar now, we shall all be hungry when winter comes."

"How can anyone kill such a boar?" one man asked bitterly. "He stands as tall as a calf, and his tusks could rip a man from thigh to shoulder at one stroke."

"I have a plan," Kunwar Lal said quietly, and he began to explain how they could end their troubles at once—and have meat for the whole village. The thought of free pork made the eyes of some of the younger men brighten; but when the plan was finally explained, no one spoke. From his hiding place Kalu listened, and he went cold with horror.

At dawn Kunwar Lal and eight other men, all armed with spears, would place themselves just outside the gap used by the wild pigs when they left their nightly feeding place. At the bottom of the field the rest of the men from the village would stand. They would be armed with any implements that could create noise.

At a given signal the noise would begin. The startled pigs would rush for the gap in the hedge. The old sow would be first, along with the piglets.

The half-grown members of the family would follow, and Burra Dhantwallah would come last. He was a good father and always made sure his family got away safely.

When he reached the gap, there would be a snare to hold him. The snare would be a stout loop of rope lying on the ground but connected to a rope which, when jerked tight, would lift the loop. This would tighten around Burra Dhantwallah's neck and hold him while the nine spearmen stabbed him to death.

There was a long silence when Kunwar Lal asked: "Who will lie alongside the hedge and pull the rope as the boar charges through? I am ready to stand in the middle of the spearmen, the most dangerous position; but there must be someone who will lie close to the hedge and pull the loop rope."

The village headman broke the silence. Soberly he asked: "Is it fair to expect any man to lie in the hedge bottom? If Burra Dhantwallah saw him, he would die without being able to rise to his feet. Do not ask me to do it, for I have a wife and children."

Kunwar Lal looked around the lamplit faces, but man after man lowered his eyes. No one would volunteer. Secretly they were hoping that before the wild pigs had eaten all the crops, they would

move on to some other place. Or perhaps the tiger would come down from the hills, snatch a piglet or two, and force the wild pigs to move.

Finally Kunwar Lal said quietly: "Very well, since none of you will help me, I shall have to ask my son to do this work. He is young, but I know he is brave. He will not refuse to help his father. Now, who will stand with me as a spearman?"

Kalu did not stay to hear the answer. He crept into his little bed and stared at the nipa-palm roof above him. He was still awake when his father and mother got into their bed, and he heard his father say: "My wife, I know there is danger for our son, as there is danger for me who will stand in the middle of the spearmen. But unless we kill this hungry boar, we shall have empty bellies next winter."

It was a long time before Kalu dropped off to sleep. He loved his father and would do anything for him; yet the thought of lying in the hedge bottom, waiting while Burra Dhantwallah and his family charged through the gap, sent shivers of fear through him.

Next morning, after his father had carefully explained how the plan would work, Kalu did not feel quite as frightened. As he walked with the village boys, following the men out to the fields, he was even proud that he had been chosen for such an important task in the plan to kill Burra Dhantwal-lah.

The wild pigs had been down to the field again, and more grain had been eaten and trampled down. Grim faced, the men turned to experiment with Kunwar Lal's idea of a foolproof plan to stop the big boar as he charged through the hedge.

A light gateway was built in the gap; and from the top a rope was suspended, on the end of which was a loop. Kalu lay by the side of the hedge, the rope tip in his hand. They got a boy to charge through the gateway, and Kalu jerked on the rope. After four attempts he got the timing right; and then six times out of six he jerked the loop up at the right instant so that the boy was caught.

A stout stake was driven into the ground so that after the boar was caught in the loop, he would be stopped as the rope tightened. The places where the spearmen would stand were marked out, and when they walked back to the village, they all looked more cheerful. The eight men who were to stand with Kalu's father got out their spears and began sharpening them. By the time they were all satisfied with their weapons, the spears had needle-sharp points.

It was while everyone was busy that an old man called Kalu aside. He was not like the other men of Chandwari Village. He was a Sikh and wore a beard which had grown long and thick. He parted it at his chin, and the ends were tied up under his big turban.

What the Sikh's full name was no one knew. He had come to Chandwari Village and asked permission to live there, saying he was a retired soldier. His pension book, which he showed proudly to the headman and the village elders, revealed that he had been a regular soldier and upon retirement had held the rank of *havildar* (sergeant). His name was Singh, but everyone knew him as Havildar since he was forever talking of the days when he had been a soldier.

Taking Kalu into his little house, he closed the door. Then from a box in the corner of the room he took a gun. It was old, yet to Kalu it looked a magnificent weapon. The wooden butt was highly polished and inlaid with silver studs, worn smooth with much polishing.

Placing it carefully on the table, Havildar Singh

said proudly: "This rifle was given to my grandfather by his father. I have always looked after it well, yet I dare not tell anyone I have it. In this land no man may own a rifle unless he has a Government license, but who would give me a license, eh?" And he shook his head before adding: "Since I am not a villager, I could not sit in the Village Council, but I listened from the shadows of a nearby house. I saw how afraid the men were when your father asked for a volunteer to work the trip rope which would snare the big boar."

Again he shook his head, then leaning forward and patting Kalu on the arm, he said: "When I heard that you were to do what the men were afraid to do, I said to myself, 'Havildar Singh, this thirteen-year-old Kalu is a brave boy and you must help him.'"

Kalu felt proud as he looked at the old Sikh. To be praised by Havildar Singh, whose war medals he had looked at and admired, made him feel stronger.

Wagging a finger at Kalu, Havildar Singh said soberly: "When you lie near the thorn hedge tomorrow, you will not feel very brave. I know this, for I was a soldier, and I know the feeling just before a battle begins. And it will be a battle tomorrow, for Burra Dhantwallah is brave. All wild boars are brave."

Kalu agreed, remembering how the big boar had turned and charged the platform after being hit by the clay balls shot at him.

"To help you," the old Sikh went on, "I shall come and lie near you, and I shall bring my rifle. If all goes well and Burra Dhantwallah is killed, I shall creep quietly away, and no one will know that I was near. If something goes wrong and you are in danger, then I shall shoot the boar."

When Kalu left Havildar Singh's house, he felt much happier. To have someone with a rifle at his side at the moment of greatest danger made him feel more confident.

Next morning while it was still dark, Kalu went with the village men along the narrow track which led to the growing crops. It was cold, and his teeth were chattering. There were others whose teeth were chattering, and not from cold. Many of the men were very frightened.

Nor did any of them feel easier when they heard, far away, a tiger calling. The tiger had been calling for several nights now, and no one could explain why. There had always been a tiger in the jungle, but it never interfered with the villagers, for there was food enough for it in the area. Yet night after night it had called. People were growing uneasy.

Just before they reached the field which the wild pigs had trampled, the men divided. One party went quietly to the bottom of Kunwar Lal's field. They carried bowls and sticks. Their task, when the right moment came, was to create as much noise as possible. They would frighten the wild pigs into headlong flight, up the slope to the gap in the thorn hedge.

The others—and Kalu was one of them—walked quietly to the gap. They checked the rope and the loop. They could hear Burra Dhantwallah and his family grunting and snuffling as they rooted up the growing grain, but for the moment it was impossible to see anything. The first faint light of the new day was only just beginning to show on the skyline of the hills to the east.

The spearmen, with Kunwar Lal in the center, settled down in the positions they had marked out the previous day. They were in a line, and each man settled down, disguised with a dark blanket over him. In the blanket was a hole through which he could see.

Kalu lay down in his place. Despite the blanket, he was cold, for a heavy dew lay on the grass, the hedge, and the sun-baked ground. For what seemed a very long time there was no sound save the first twitterings of bird life as the new day slowly brightened.

Kalu twitched nervously as he sensed something behind him. Then he felt Havildar Singh's hand on his back and heard the whisper: "I am with you, Kalu, and my rifle is loaded. This is the worst time —waiting. Once the battle begins, you will forget your fears."

The day began to grow brighter. Then the first yellow light shone on the tops of trees across the valley. The sun was rising above the distant hills. At once there was a yell from the bottom of the field. The headman was signaling for the noise to begin.

The quietness of the new day was shattered as men began to bang on brass bowls and gongs, yelling as loud as they could. Led by the headman, they began to trot up the field.

Kalu gripped the rope so tightly that his knuckles showed white under the chocolate-colored skin. Havildar Singh laid a hand on Kalu's back. "Steady, Kalu. Remember, the big boar will come last of all."

Lying on the ground, Kalu felt the small vibrations as the wild pigs galloped up the field, their hard hoofs hammering the baked earth like the hoofs of a brigade of cavalry.

Kalu lifted himself on one elbow. His father and the other spearmen were still huddled under their blankets, staring through their spy holes. They were waiting for the sow and younger pigs to pass through the gap. Then when the big boar came charging through, they would rise.

First through the gap came the old sow, mother of the family, and with her the young piglets squeaking in panic. At sight of the nine blanket-covered men the sow swerved, and the piglets with her. Next came the half-grown members of the family—sows and young boars. They too swerved aside and went crashing up the bush-covered slope which led to safety.

Last of all came the big boar. Kalu saw him through a tiny gap in the thorn hedge. He had been eating young corn, and there was a fleck of green foam on his lips. The first pale gold of the sun shone on his tusks, giving them a warm ivory color. Yet they looked like terrible weapons.

"Ready?" Havildar Singh asked. At that same

moment Kalu's father rose, and throwing off his blanket, he yelled: "Now, Kalu!"

Kalu did not see the other eight spearmen throw off their blankets and leap to their feet, spears ready. He gave a short, sharp jerk on the rope. There was a click as the wooden peg which held the big noose was pulled out and the loop dropped down.

As Burra Dhantwallah rushed on, he drew the rope tight, and the noose was drawn firmly about his throat. There was a twang as the rope was pulled taut under the boar's weight, and a moment later Burra Dhantwallah was almost jerked over backward. He was lifted up until his short front legs were pawing the air, and his whole chest and belly were exposed for the spear thrusts. Kalu's father stepped forward, his spear drawn back. Then the unexpected happened.

The rope did not break—but under the sudden strain the wooden post which was to anchor it to the ground broke. With part of the stake still fastened, the end of the rope swept around like a whip. As it did so, Burra Dhantwallah dropped down onto all four feet again. He was grunting with rage, and he had eyes only for the line of men

facing him. He shot forward almost as though he had been flung from a catapult, and the line broke.

With a screech of terror, one man panicked and turned to run. The man who fled unnerved the

others. All but Kunwar Lal turned and leaped for their lives. Now it was one man against a boar. Kalu's father stepped forward, his spear leveled to take the charging boar.

Disaster

Left foot well forward to give him perfect balance, Kalu's father stabbed down with all his strength. He was aiming for a spot behind the boar's head. If the steel had gone home in the right spot, Burra Dhantwallah would have died instantly.

The boar was no clumsy old pig. All his life he had been the one who had fought for his family. He was a warrior; and quick as a flash when he saw the glint of steel, he swung his massive head to one side.

The needle-sharp point of the spear, which should have gone deep into the back of his neck, merely grazed his cheek and went into his shoulder. Even then he was lucky, for the spear struck his shoulder blade instead of driving deep into his heart or lungs.

If he felt the pain he did not show it, but continued his charge. Kalu's father, gripping the spear shaft tightly, was thrown backward. Too late he loosened his grip on the spear shaft and reeled wildly in an effort to regain his balance and leap to safety.

Burra Dhantwallah was too quick for him. Kalu's father was tossed into the air, then struck the dusty ground and rolled over, face down. In his wild rage the boar raced past him, trailing the rope which had first checked his bid for safety.

Wheeling around with amazing speed, he raked angrily at one of the blankets lying on the ground, tossing it into the air. He was looking for his enemy; and as he tossed another blanket only five or six feet from where Kunwar Lal lay, Kalu darted forward, screaming.

He had no weapon and was even smaller than his father. His only chance was to grab the rope looped tightly about the boar's neck and try to drag Burra Dhantwallah away. He grabbed the end, with its broken piece of stake still attached, and jerked frantically. He looped the rope around his right wrist and tried to keep the boar away from the fallen man.

The moment the rope tightened, Kalu was

brought to a stop. Ten boys of his size and weight
could not have dragged Burra Dhantwallah. His
eyes blazing with pain and anger, the boar stood
for a moment as he looked around for the man he
knew he had hurt.

Kalu screamed at him and pulled hard on the rope. The jerk tightened the loop around Burra Dhantwallah's neck, impeding his breathing. At this extra pressure the boar turned and saw Kalu. Giving a half squeal, half grunt, he charged at the boy.

Kalu could not move. Like someone suddenly turned to stone, he waited, and at that instant there was an explosion. It was not like a gunshot. It was an ear-splitting roar—like a charge of dynamite exploding in free air. Its effect on the boar was amazing. He was within six feet of Kalu when the thunderous bellow shocked the eardrums of all who were near. Burra Dhantwallah's hoofs dug into the yellow soil, throwing up spurts of dust. He slithered to a stop less than a yard from Kalu, then wheeled like a ballet dancer and rushed away, making for the scrub-covered hillside and the safety of the family lair on the hilltop.

As Burra Dhantwallah raced away, the rope tightened about his neck; and the other end, which was looped about Kalu's wrist, dragged the boy forward. Losing his balance, Kalu sprawled full length; and as he struck the ground, he tried to let go the rope. But it would not go free.

For a few seconds he was dragged across the ground. Then he swung his left hand across to his right wrist, hoping to loosen the coiled rope. It was impossible. Burra Dhantwallah was racing for safety as fast as his sturdy legs would take him, and the rope kept far too taut for Kalu to ease it free.

Fighting to keep his body off the ground, Kalu did not feel the pain as the skin was burned off his knees and elbows. There were bushes ahead, and if he was dragged into one of them, he might die impaled on a branch.

The boar also had to face the bushes; and when he had to swing to one side to avoid one, it gave Kalu a chance. As the rope slackened for an instant, he managed to leap to his feet. There was no time to fumble with the rope around his wrist. The rope tightened again as the boar rushed on, and Kalu had to follow, bounding along in frantic leaps.

There were low bushes to avoid, for the boar swung easily around these, but the rope brushed into them. Kalu had to leap over the smaller ones and somehow swing around the larger bushes.

Burra Dhantwallah was slowing down, for the rope with which he was dragging Kalu was tightening under the constant pressure. The boar was finding it more and more difficult to breathe. Only his tremendous courage kept him going. He wanted to reach his family before he died.

Ahead was an enormous bush. The boar swung sharp left, then sharp right, causing the rope connecting him to Kalu to swing into the branches.

Suddenly the bush began to shake as though a giant hand was heaving at it. The rope had slid between two branches and down to a point where the gap was very small. For a second, smoke spurted up as the rope was drawn through the narrow gap by the sheer weight and strength of Burra Dhantwallah. Then it jammed tight.

Again Burra Dhantwallah was jerked back onto his haunches, and the loop about his neck was pulled even tighter. His grunt of anger was reduced to a throaty gurgle, but he was not going to surrender. He got his balance, paused for a second, then gave a mighty bound forward. The rope could not withstand that strain, and it broke.

With the noose even tighter about his neck, each breath the boar took was an agony. He made a thin whistling noise as he sucked in air, and when he finally reached the hilltop where his family was gathered, even his sturdy legs were shaking so badly that he collapsed, and the old sow nosed at him anxiously.

A younger boar, one of Dhantwallah's sons, began to chew at the rope about his father's neck. Within minutes, at the cost of some skin, the rope was gnawed through. But Burra Dhantwallah was almost at Death's door when the rope fell away, allowing him to breathe freely again.

Much farther down the slope Kalu was lying spread-eagled under the bush into which he had been dragged. His hand was swollen and blue, and when he loosened the tight coils of rope, the pain made him moan in agony as blood began to circulate again.

The sun was now well above the hilltops. Birds were flying backward and forward, insects droned to and fro in the short sun-dried grass beneath the bushes, but Kalu hardly heard them. Once the pain in his right wrist began to ease, he closed his eyes and dropped off into a deep, soothing sleep. Nor did he lift his head or open his eyes when far down the slope someone began calling his name.

Again and again the unseen caller broke the quiet with a repeated shrill: "Kalu! Kalu! Kalu!" Kalu did not move, and the first he knew of the searcher was when gentle hands turned him over onto his back. As he opened his eyes, he looked into the anxious face of Havildar Singh.

"I knew you were not dead," the old man croaked. "They all said you must be dead, or you would have come back. Have you any broken bones?"

Kalu eased himself into a sitting position. Every part of his body seemed to be bruised, yet he forgot his own pain when he looked again at Havildar Singh. He hardly recognized him.

He who had always been so proud of his fine silvery beard now had only half a beard, with a huge blister from cheek to temple. His bushy eyebrows were gone.

"What has happened to you?" Kalu asked.

The Sikh shook his head sadly. "My rifle, which I have looked after so carefully—alas, it burst when I tried to shoot that *shaitan* (devil) of a boar. I am lucky I was not blinded, and . . . but what am I doing wasting time? Kalu, are you able to walk back to the village? Your father needs you. He needs you very much."

"He is badly hurt?"

"You must get back to him at once," Havildar Singh said hurriedly, "or he will be in great danger."

Kalu groaned as he started to struggle to his feet. Every muscle felt as stiff as a board, and even a slight movement produced agonizing pain. There were tears in his eyes when he looked up at the old man and muttered: "I'm sorry, Mr. Singh, I cannot do it."

"You must do it," Havildar Singh insisted. "The boar ripped open your father's leg from knee to thigh. And though we have cleansed the wound and wrapped it in clean rags, he must go to the hospital. It must be stitched by a doctor and disinfected, or there could be blood poisoning. And he will not leave his house until he knows you are safe," Havildar Singh explained. " 'Bring my only son to me. Then I will go to the hospital.' That was what he said."

Making a mighty effort, Kalu got to his feet. But when he tried to walk, he had to grab at the old man for support.

"Stand still for a moment," Havildar Singh said gently. "I shall carry you. Among the medals pinned on my best coat is one to remind me of the day when I carried a full-grown man, a white officer. Then the guns were roaring, and all about me men were dying."

Dropping to one knee, he ordered Kalu to drape

himself over his shoulder. Then Havildar Singh began the greatest rescue of his entire life. He was an
old man, the way was rough, and the village was
more than half a mile distant. By the time he

reached the village well, he was tottering and glad enough to let two women take Kalu from him.

The women would have taken the boy straight to his home, but even in his panting, exhausted state, Havildar Singh waved an arm and shook his head. "No," he gasped. "He must be washed and given clean clothing."

The women spent several minutes cleaning up Kalu and finding fresh clothing for him. Then they carried him to the door of the house. By this time the old Sikh had recovered enough to take charge. He laid a hand on Kalu's shoulder. "You must walk in yourself," he whispered. "No limping, no sign of pain. It is a battle you are fighting for your father's life."

Kalu's mother gave a great wail at the sight of him and burst into tears. Like most of the people of the village, she had been certain her son was dead. A number of the villagers had seen Kalu being dragged behind Burra Dhantwallah, and all had been sure the great boar had killed him.

Kunwar Lal lay on his string bed, one leg a mass of makeshift bandages. He took Kalu's hands and gripped them weakly. "Now I can go to the hospital with an easy mind," he said. "But try, my son, not to let the pigs eat up what remains of our crop.

If they do, we shall starve when winter comes."

"When you come back from the hospital, Father, there shall not be a Dhantwallah to eat anyone's crops," Kalu promised.

At these words Kalu's mother gazed at him in horror, afraid of what might happen to her son. If it had been possible to kill the big boar, Kalu's father would have done it. Instead, he was lying here, badly injured. In his weak state, however, Kunwar Lal was ready to believe anything. He smiled as he gripped Kalu's hands again. Then, looking across at the village headman, he said shakily: "Now I am ready to go to the hospital, Headman. And the quicker the better."

Within minutes everything was ready for the thirty-mile journey. There had been many volunteers to carry the injured man. The eight spearmen who had deserted Kunwar Lal in the moment of danger were eager to wipe out the memory of their cowardice. A comfortable stretcher had been made; and when the men started off, Kalu's mother walked behind. On her head she carried a large bundle containing food, cooking pots, and clothing.

When they reached the hospital, she would

make a small shelter for herself in the grounds, and live there. She would have to take food in each day for her husband until he was fit enough to come home. In these small Indian hospitals it was impossible to provide food for the patients. If Kalu's mother spent what little money she took with her, then she would have to try to get work nearby; but she would stay with her husband until he was fit to travel back to Chandwari Village.

Kalu stood outside their house as his father was carried away. He blinked hard to stop the tears overflowing onto his cheeks. Until his father returned, he was the man of the house.

The village headman came up to him and spoke gently: "Your father will get well quicker now that he thinks there is no danger to his crops. That was a brave lie you told, Kalu. I think such lies can be forgiven."

Kalu swallowed the lump in his throat. Turning to the headman, he said in a voice which trembled: "It was not a lie. I *am* going to kill the big boar. He has hurt my father, and I shall kill him."

The headman nodded, though he did not believe Kalu meant what he said. No boy, however brave, would dare tackle Burra Dhantwallah.

Kalu must be stopped!

When Kalu hobbled back into the house, the whole village was feeling sorry for him. One man followed him into the house to assure him that if he needed any help with the weeding or with their two cows and six goats, he would get one of his sons to help.

A neighboring woman went into her little kitchen, blew the smoldering embers of her cooking fire into a blaze, and began to prepare some food. She knew that Kalu had not eaten anything since the evening meal the previous day.

Kalu was lying on his bed when the woman came in with a platter of smoking *chapattis* (pancakes), some hot spices, and a bowl of cool milk. "Until your father and mother return," the woman said, "you can have food from my cooking fire anytime, Kalu."

Kalu's next visitor was Havildar Singh, and he carried an armful of plants which he had gathered from the rough ground behind the village. They were *Brahm Buti* (God's flower) plants, and the villagers used them for curing cuts and sores.

"It will be three days before you are fit to walk again," the old man said cheerily as he began twisting and crushing the plants to make them give off the healing sap. "Lie still, and when I have finished, it will be time for you to sleep."

"But there are the cows and goats to bring in and milk," Kalu protested. "And they must be taken to water before sunset. Besides, I cannot lie here for three days. That *shaitan* (devil) Burra Dhantwallah will have eaten all our field bare in three days' time."

"The cows and goats shall be seen to," was Havildar Singh's calm reply. "As for the boar, we shall talk of killing him later. Now is the time for healing. Lie still."

"But I . . ." Kalu protested.

"Lie still," Havildar Singh said again, and when Kalu still refused to lie down, the old man repeated his command in a soldier's parade ground voice.

"LIE STILL!" The bellow made Kalu's eyes open wide, but this time he obeyed.

With a smile on his face and twinkling eyes, Havildar Singh said: "One of the things a soldier learns is that a man who is tired, sore, or injured cannot fight anyone and win. We shall get you fit again—then deal with the big boar."

"How?" Kalu asked anxiously. He had insisted that he would kill Burra Dhantwallah, but so far he had no definite plan in mind.

Havildar Singh would not make any suggestion beyond "I shall think, Kalu. At the end of three days, if you have rested and let me deal with your bruises, then I shall tell you what I have thought up."

On the morning of the fourth day, Havildar Singh gave Kalu his idea for killing Burra Dhant-wallah.

"The pigs always enter your father's field at the same place," the old man began. "If we dug a pit across the opening—a deep pit—and one or two pigs fell in, the others would be frightened and would not come to your father's field again."

"They would see the pit," Kalu said promptly. "Even at dusk they would see the hole and go around it. And there is another thing. If they stopped feeding on my father's crops, they would go to the fields of other villagers."

"You did not let me finish talking," Havildar Singh pointed out gently. "After digging the pit, we would cover the top with a layer of thin bamboo. Over that we would sprinkle earth and dead grass. With dusk turning to darkness, even a pig as clever as Burra Dhantwallah would not realize we had set a trap."

"Ah, if we could trap the big boar," Kalu sighed. "That would be enough. His family would leave the area at once. Could we catch him, Mr. Singh?"

"I think so," was the confident reply. "I have heard men wise in the ways of animals say that the wild boar is the bravest father, and the kindliest. He will always lead if there is danger, and always bring up the rear when the family is being pursued. He would be the first to enter the field at night."

"Digging a pit would not be easy," Kalu murmured after thinking over the idea.

"I shall speak to the headman," Havildar Singh said confidently. "He will want his share of the meat when we carry the dead boar home, so he must help in the preparations. Rest here, and I will speak to him."

The Sikh asked the village headman if he would call a meeting that night to discuss a plan he had for killing Burra Dhantwallah.

"We listened to poor Kunwar Lal's plan," the headman reminded Havildar Singh. "Look what happened to him."

"In my plan no one will be near enough to be injured," Havildar Singh assured him. And refusing to say anything more, he left the headman to call the meeting.

Because he did not really belong to Chandwari Village, Havildar Singh was not allowed to speak at the Village Council, so Kalu was called to explain the plan. He told the circle of men how they would dig the deep pit and cover it with bamboo so thin it would not support even a small wild pig. Later they would have to kill their prisoner in the pit and carry it home.

When Kalu had finished, the headman asked him to leave the Council for a few minutes while he and the older men discussed the idea. When he was called back, Kalu's heart sank when he saw the solemn expression on the faces of the men.

"We have considered your idea," the headman said. "It is not a good idea. All you will succeed in doing is frightening Burra Dhantwallah and his family away from your father's field and into the fields of other villagers. Your father's crop is almost ruined, and it is better that the pigs should continue to feed there. We have agreed to give your father a small share of each man's crop, but you must not try to kill the boar. You couldn't do it anyway."

"But when the pigs have eaten all our crops, they will surely visit the fields of other men," Kalu protested. "If we dug a pit . . ." and there the headman stopped him.

"We have all heard the tiger which has been calling in the hills for the past week. We have given gifts to the temple, and the priest has prayed for the tiger to come down and kill some of the pigs. If that happens, the rest of the *sounder* (family) of pigs will go away."

Kalu stared at the circle of grave-faced village men. The pigs had not broken into their fields, and harvest time was only five or six weeks away. They did not want the wild pigs frightened off their present feeding ground and into other fields.

Pointing an angry finger at the headman, Kalu

shouted: "I promised my father that I would kill Burra Dhantwallah. What will I say to him when he returns from the hospital and finds his crop eaten away? He will ask me why I did not keep my promise."

"Your father will not blame you," the headman said soothingly. "Since *he* could not kill the big boar, how could he expect a small boy like you to kill it?"

"I have not yet tried," said Kalu. "It will be time to say I have failed when the pit does not trap Burra Dhantwallah. After I have dug the pit . . ."

The rest of his words were drowned by an angry uproar from the villagers. The headman waved his arms for silence, and when he could be heard, he walked across to Kalu. He wagged a warning finger only inches from the boy's face and said shrilly: "There is to be no digging anywhere. The Village Council has decided that. If you try to dig, you will be punished."

"And tell that old fool Havildar Singh that if he tries, he will be punished as well," a gray-bearded man yelled. "We know he has been with you every day since your father was taken to the hospital. He is not one of us, and it will be easy enough to put fire to his house if he persuades you to dig a pit. Tell him that. I don't like Sikhs anyway, and the sooner he leaves this village, the better."

Kalu jumped to his feet and ran down the darkened village street to his house. He was almost crying with vexation. The plan Havildar Singh had thought up seemed such a good one.

When he rushed into the house and flung himself on his creaking little bed, there was a movement from the darkest corner, and a moment later the old Sikh came over to kneel by the bedside.

"I listened to them," he said quietly. "A man doesn't need to attend a meeting when the men are angry. They shout so that their voices go to the very rooftops. So you are not to dig the pit, Kalu."

Kalu sat up. "I *am* going to dig a pit," he said angrily. "I promised my father that I would get rid of the boar, and I will. I shall dig the pit myself."

For perhaps twenty seconds there was silence in the hot little room, and then Havildar Singh spoke. "I am a Sikh, and we Sikhs are fighting men. If you mean to dig a pit for Burra Dhantwallah, then I am willing to help you. Sit up. A boy with his face hidden in a blanket cannot talk as men talk. Men look at one another when they talk. I am an old man, you are a young man. Let us talk of this pit digging. When shall we begin?"

They decided they must start next morning before dawn and be well on with the work before anyone knew of it. After Havildar Singh went over to his house, Kalu lay down to stare into the darkness of the roof until he dropped off to sleep. His sleep was troubled with dreams, and in the middle of the dreams was a giant wild boar with tusks as large as the tusks of an elephant.

An hour before the first sign of dawn, Havildar Singh crept into Kalu's bedroom carrying a cup of smoking tea. It was one of the luxuries the old man allowed himself. Tea-drinking was a habit he had learned while serving with a regiment whose officers were British. That was many years ago, but the tea-drinking habit had remained with him.

They drank their tea and ate some chapattis with *ghee* (rancid butter). Then they moved quietly out into the coolness which always comes just before dawn. A pi-dog sneaked out from behind a house, teeth bared, but it scuttled back when Kalu snapped a threat at it. These pi-dogs, which belonged to nobody and lived by picking over the rubbish heaps, were cowards at heart; and no village boy was afraid of them.

Kalu carried a shovel and his father's spear. There was a dull brick-red stain on the spear point which Kalu refused to clean off. It was the blood of Burra Dhantwallah, a reminder that Kalu's father had faced the boar.

As they drew near the field where the crops had been partially eaten, a tiger called. It was the same calling that had alarmed the villagers for a week now. It was not the call a tiger makes when seeking a mate. It was almost as if the animal was in pain.

"If that tiger would come down here some evening," Havildar Singh said, pausing to listen to the tiger as it called again, "it could eat well and save us a lot of trouble. Digging a pit will not be easy."

"Would a tiger face Burra Dhantwallah?" Kalu asked. "I have heard the old men say that only a half-starved tiger would face a wild boar."

He got no answer to his question for just then, ahead, they heard the patter of a hundred small hoofs. Burra Dhantwallah had heard the voices, and he was leading his family out of the field and back up the hill earlier than usual. He was less confident since he had been half strangled by the rope around his neck.

"Tonight will be the last time he will try to enter my father's field," Kalu promised. "How happy I would be if we could kill him. Then I could look my father in the face, and he would know that he has a son who keeps his word."

"Perhaps we shall kill him," the old Sikh said, throwing his spade down. "But now we must wait until there is a little light so that we can mark off the size of the pit."

They marked out the pit as soon as the gray of dawn began to creep over the distant hills. By the time the sun rose, they were digging furiously; and when the first golden light tipped the treetops, boy and man were wet with perspiration. The morning was as cool as usual, but the work was difficult. The soil was baked hard by the sun, and it was full of stones. The pit, which was to stretch right across the gap in the thorn hedge, was eight feet long and six feet wide. It had to be that wide to prevent Burra Dhantwallah from leaping over it.

"How deep?" Kalu asked, wiping the sweat from his brow as they rested for a few moments.

"Deeper than a tall man," Havildar Singh said. "A wild boar is a very determined animal, and once he is in the pit, we must not have him climbing out."

An hour after the sun rose, they heard the lowing of cattle and the chatter of young voices. They knew what that meant. Two or three of the village boys were driving the cows out to the usual grazing spot. This was a place where an underground spring welled up, and spreading outward, it kept a patch of grass always green and luscious, no matter how hot and dry the summer had been.

The cows walked placidly past the two diggers, but the three village boys gaped in astonishment. Though none of them had been at the meeting of the Village Council, they all knew what had been said. While the village men sat in a ring, their faces lit by a small lamp, women and inquisitive children lurked in the shadows of the nearby houses and listened. As a result, everyone knew that Kalu had been forbidden to dig a pit.

Kalu paused for a moment as the boys drew level. Leaning on his spade he said: "When you bring the cows back this afternoon, be sure to take them farther up the hill. We don't want a cow falling into the pit. They won't see it, for it will be covered with earth and grass."

The three boys nodded and walked on for a few yards before stopping and looking back. Some conversation passed between them. Then two boys

went on after the cows, but the third ran past the
partly-dug hole and back toward the village.

"Thus does trouble begin for us," Havildar
Singh said heavily. "The boy has gone to tell the
headman that you and I are disobeying the orders
of the Village Council. Now we really must dig

and get as deep as we can before angry men come to stop us. They will be like hornets waiting to sting somebody."

The old Sikh was right. Within half an hour, while he and Kalu were still deepening the pit as quickly as they could, they heard the sound of voices. The headman with about twenty of the village men surrounded the pit, and Kalu looked up as the headman yelled angrily: "What did I tell you last night, Kalu Lal?"

Kalu looked sideways at Havildar Singh, who drew all eyes on himself when he said laughingly: "I did not think you had such a poor memory, Mr. Headman. I was not at the meeting, but I heard you shouting to Kalu. You said that neither he nor that old fool Havildar Singh must dig a hole, or they would be punished. Is that not what you said?"

"You may think that is a joke, Havildar Singh," the angry headman snapped, "but I have an answer to jokes like that. From this day you are not welcome in the village of Chandwari. You repay our kindness by helping this stupid boy defy the Village Council, and that is our way of repaying you."

"I am trying to help the boy," Havildar Singh said. "Is it wrong to help someone?"

"We said the hole must not be dug, and that is

the finish of it." Looking past Havildar Singh, he said: "Kalu, I order you to start filling in this hole at once."

Kalu's heart was thumping, but he shook his head. "I am digging the hole in my father's land."

Stepping to one side, the headman motioned to several of the younger men. "Get him out," he ordered, "and then fill in the hole."

Unexpected trouble

Four of the young men stepped forward, but they stopped on the brink of the pit, for Havildar Singh had grabbed the spear Kalu had brought along. Holding it as a soldier holds a rifle with the bayonet fixed, he menaced the four.

"Get back," he ordered, and jabbed threateningly at the nearest when there was no response to his command. At that, all four stepped back, and Havildar Singh scrambled out of the pit. "I have been a soldier all my life, friends," he said. "I am a man of peace, but I have always been ready to defend those who could not defend themselves. If you . . ."

There was a movement in the crowd, and a man tossed a stone toward Havildar Singh. If he had not

stepped quickly to one side, it would have struck
him in the face.

"Stone them," the man yelled, stooping for another stone.

Kalu cringed in the pit, for the stone had nar-
rowly missed him. He looked up in time to see

Havildar Singh take a quick step forward. He thrust his spear point until it was within inches of the headman's chest, and said sternly: "I think it will be better if you step into the pit with me. If the Village Council decides to kill us with stones, they can kill you as well."

The headman's eyes went glassy, but he stepped forward, halting at the brink of the pit as Havildar Singh moved to one side.

"Well," the Sikh demanded, "is there to be stoning or no stoning?"

"There will be no stoning," the headman babbled. "I would never allow it, never."

"Then send these men back, and if you have not yet eaten, a boy can bring you food and drink," Havildar Singh said coldly. "You are staying here until we have dug this pit."

"You will pay for this," a man at the back of the crowd threatened.

"I am always ready to pay," the old man retorted. "Why don't you at the back come forward and meet me face to face? They say it is the dog at the back that yaps loudest and runs first when there is danger. If you are not a coward, come forward and meet me."

There was no reply from the man who had

thrown the stone, and after a moment someone chuckled.

Kalu stepped out of the pit, saying: "Let our headman go, Mr. Singh. He is a man to be trusted. If he says there will be no stoning, there will be no stoning."

Havildar Singh lowered the spear point, and with a sigh of relief the headman backed away. His face was covered with perspiration. He had had a fright he would not forget for a long time. Without a word he pushed his way through the small crowd and headed back to the village. The rest of the men followed him, muttering to one another. Like their headman, they would not forget this. Since the headman had said there would be no stoning, they would obey, but they were promising one another that Havildar Singh would pay for what he had done. At least they could drive him out of the village.

When all was quiet again, the old man returned to the pit; but as he picked up his spade, Kalu said sadly: "I am very sorry this happened, Mr. Singh. They will not forgive you and may drive you out of Chandwari."

"There are other villages," the old man pointed out, "and I have been without friends before. I have my army pension, and a man with money is usually welcome anywhere. I shall be sorry to leave, for I was beginning to make friends in Chandwari."

There was a note of sadness in his voice. While he had doctored Kalu's wounds, the old man had talked about his past—how he had retired from the army and lived happily for a few years with his wife and grown-up children until cholera broke out. Havildar Singh had been inoculated against the terrible disease while a soldier, but his wife and his married sons and their wives had never been inoculated. The disease had taken them all; and to forget his sorrows, Havildar Singh had packed a few things into an old army backpack and wandered off, finally coming to Chandwari.

In silence boy and man worked throughout the rest of the morning and part of the afternoon. They dug the pit eight feet long, six feet wide, and six feet deep. The sides were straight so that it would be difficult for any animal to get out.

When the digging was finished, they cut bamboos, split them, and laid them across the pit top. Then they covered the bamboo with a sprinkling of soil and dead grass. Tired but satisfied with their hard work, Kalu and Havildar Singh stood and examined the trap top. Then they turned and nodded to each other. A man might be suspicious, but an animal would never suspect there was a deep pit below the dead grass.

When they got back to the village, the women were busy preparing the evening meal. No one spoke to them, for the women knew what had happened. They must not show any sign of friendliness until the trouble had blown over.

"Come and eat with me," Havildar Singh suggested, "for it is as easy to cook for two as for one, and we need only light one fire."

Kalu brought water so they could wash, and while Havildar Singh lit the fire and began making chapattis, Kalu went for milk. They were tired, but they had done a good day's work, and by morning might well have Burra Dhantwallah in the pit.

Outside, the sunlight was losing some of its rich gold as the day drew to an end. The bird which men called the whistling schoolboy flew over the village, and that was always a sign of approaching sunset.

Cattle and goats began wandering into the village as boys brought them in for the night. With a heap of steaming chapattis in front of them, Kalu and Havildar Singh were eating when the chatter of the village street suddenly stopped.

In the quiet a boy could be heard shouting, a sound which started the pi-dogs barking furiously and brought a chorus of startled inquiries from women hurrying to their doors.

"Perhaps Burra Dhantwallah has come down early and fallen into the pit," Kalu suggested, but he did not really believe that.

Havildar Singh shook his head and made for the open door. "The boar is not such a fool, Kalu. In any case, the boy would be shouting with joy. That shouting is from fear. Something has gone wrong. Finish your meal. I'll see."

There was a growing clamor in the village street now, and Kalu's heart sank as he detected anger in the voices and heard his name mentioned. Bolting the mouthful of chapatti he had been chewing, he joined the old man at the door. He stared down the dirt-paved street at a growing crowd of men, women, and boys. In front was the village headman and with him a boy whose face was wet with tears.

"I asked you not to dig that pit!" the headman yelled. "Your pit has worked—but not with the big boar! Do you know what animal is trapped in your pit?"

Kalu guessed the answer even before Havildar Singh could ask: "What?" The boy whose face was wet with tears was one of the three who had driven cows past the pit that morning.

The boys had not forgotten the warning Kalu had given them, but one of the cows had suddenly ambled down the hillside, making for the track they always used. Nor could she be driven uphill again. Yelling and whacking her across her bony hips, the boys had tried to drive her uphill, but she had suddenly raced ahead. Before they could control her, she had plunged onto the flimsy carpet of bamboo and earth which hid the pit.

One terrifying thought had turned Kalu's heart to ice. Suppose the cow died! Cows were sacred animals. If this one died, the consequences would be too terrible to think of. Not only would there be compensation to the owner of the animal, but there would be penance to make for committing such a crime.

In the midst of his fears, Kalu heard Havildar Singh say calmly: "The pit is not so deep that we cannot haul the cow out. If you and some of the men will help us, Mr. Headman, we can rescue the cow, and I will pay you all a little something when next I go for my army pension."

"But the sun is already starting to set," the headman protested. "And what about the tiger which has been calling all the past week. The bawling of a cow will surely bring it down and . . ."

"We could take lights . . . lamps and torches," Havildar Singh suggested. "Does a tiger come where there are lights and voices? No! We can forget the tiger. I will fill my own lamp, and if others will bring lamps, and the boys cut bamboo for torches, we could have the cow back in the village within the hour. And don't forget, Mr. Headman, I will reward everyone who helps when I next draw my pension. Maybe half a rupee for each man."

There was silence at that. Money was scarce in Chandwari, and even half a rupee was well worth picking up for an hour's work. Then one or two of the women began to protest that the evening meal was almost ready for eating, and in any case it was madness to go out to the fields when the day was ending.

"Let those who dig the pit get the cow out," a man shouted. He was the one who had thrown the stone.

Havildar Singh had a quick answer. "There are cowards in this village, I know, Headman. But you are not a coward. You and I and young Kalu, together with half a dozen of the younger men, can rescue the cow in an hour. Come." In a whisper to the headman so that no one else could hear, he added: "There will be two rupees for you when my pension comes."

The headman was not eager to go, but neither did he want to be thought a coward. And the two rupees helped him make up his mind. After a moment he gruffly ordered his wife to bring their biggest lamp. A number of younger men hurried off for lamps, and within ten minutes the rescue party was ready. They had lamps, bamboo for torches, and ropes. One young man brought a four-gallon gasoline tin which his wife used for carrying water. By beating on that with a short iron spike, he could make plenty of noise.

With the sun setting and the first stars showing dimly in the east, no one wanted to be away from the village. The trapped cow was bawling, and that was sure to attract a tiger or a leopard.

When the group reached the last cultivated field and crowded round the pit, the sun had set and the sky to the west was a deep purple-red. In that part of India the time between sunset and darkness is very short, and night seems to fall like a curtain being drawn across a window.

The cow lay in the pit bottom, and her eyes shone luminescent in the light from the lamps

shining round the pit top. Comforted by the presence of men, the cow stopped bawling and waited for someone to help her. The man who owned the cow called on her to stand up.

She was a splendid three-year-old beast, and in full milk. She began to struggle as her owner coaxed her to stand, but when she was almost upright, she flopped sideways. One of the older men gave a yelp of dismay, and then pointing down, he said: "The left back leg . . . it is broken. I saw it. It is broken."

The murmur of voices died away, and all eyes turned on the headman. If the cow had a broken leg, then they might as well go home. The beast would surely die. No one could imagine a broken leg mending.

"I'll get down and look," Kalu volunteered.

A younger man helped Kalu slide down into the pit. A lamp was lowered to him, and carefully stepping round the fallen cow, he bent to examine the back legs.

A moment later Kalu was forgotten as from somewhere in the nearby jungle a barking deer called. The animal may have been a hundred yards away or quarter of a mile—it was hard to tell. In the stillness which falls over the land at dusk, sound carries great distances. The barking made everyone around the pit stiffen and look out into the gathering gloom.

The barking deer was the jungle watchman. It called to warn others that a meat-eater was prowling, usually a tiger or a leopard.

The headman turned, and looking into the pit, he asked anxiously: "Well, Kalu, is the leg broken or not?"

Kalu swallowed the lump in his throat. He had seen the leg, and it was broken about ten inches above the cloven hoof. He nodded and pointed, then lowered the lamp close to the leg so that those on the ground above could see.

"Yes, it is broken," the headman muttered, and he sounded relieved. "In that case we may as well go home. We could never get a cow with a broken leg back to the village. Come on, Kalu, let me help you up." Dropping to one knee, he stretched out a hand to give Kalu a heave upward.

Kalu started to raise his right hand, then lowered it. If they left the cow, then it surely would die. It would begin its frightened lowing once more, and that would bring the tiger along. The result for his father, if the cow died, was too terrible to contemplate.

"Come on, boy, come on," the headman snapped impatiently. "We don't want to stay here any longer than is necessary. You heard the barking deer. That means the tiger is probably not far away. Give me your hand."

"Pass down the ropes," Kalu said urgently. "I will put them under the cow and then we can haul her up."

"Haul her up! Don't be a fool!" The headman sounded exasperated. "What is the use of dragging her out of the pit when she has a broken leg? She will die anyway."

"Broken legs have been mended," Havildar Singh protested. "Let us get the cow and . . ."

"If we try to move her, she will start making a row," the headman said angrily. "And that could bring the tiger. If . . . there you are, the barking deer calls again. The tiger is near." Leaning over the pit, he looked down at Kalu and asked: "Are you coming or not? We are going back to the village."

"I'm not leaving the cow," Kalu protested. "My father will have to pay for her and also do penance for the priest who will say we killed the animal."

"You did kill her," the headman snapped. "You

dug the pit, and the blame is on you. Now, are you coming back with us or not? I am not staying to wait for the tiger."

"I am staying," Kalu said. There was a tremble in his voice.

"We'll leave you," the headman threatened, and as the barking deer called again, and this time the call sounded more urgent, several of the villagers turned down the track toward the village. The man with the gasoline can started to make a noise, thumping the can with all his strength.

As the villagers departed, the headman turned to Havildar Singh. "You are friendly with the boy," he said in a pleading voice. "Get him to go home. That tiger may be coming here at this moment." There was no disguising the fear in the headman's voice.

"He's determined to stay, Mr. Headman," Havildar Singh said soberly. "And since one cannot leave a boy alone, even if he is a fool, I will stay with him. Will you come and see what has happened in the morning?"

The headman looked hard at the old Sikh, then nodded. "I will do that, Havildar Singh, and I just hope I find you both alive. You are a brave man, though I think you are a fool. You are risking your life for a boy who is surely mad." Then he picked up his lantern and ran after the others.

Havildar Singh watched the bobbing lantern until it was lost to sight. From the darkness of the jungle the call of the barking deer came again.

A tiger!

Havildar Singh lowered himself over the edge of the pit, and with Kalu's hands to guide his feet, he dropped down alongside the cow.

"You heard the barking deer?" he suggested, and nodded grimly when Kalu agreed that he had.

"But I can't let the cow die," Kalu said anxiously. "It is a great sin to kill a cow, and if she dies, I shall be blamed."

The Sikh nodded agreement. He knew that the law does not punish the killer of a cow, but the village priest would inflict punishment. This could mean a gift of money to the temple, something Kalu's father could not afford. Also Kalu might have to make a pilgrimage to a distant holy place. Since he was too young to make such a pilgrimage on his own, his father would have to accompany him. His mother would be left behind to care for their cows and goats, as well as look after the remains of their crops.

"I heard you say that broken legs could be mended." Kalu looked hopefully at Havildar Singh. "Could we not mend the cow's leg?"

The old Sikh leaned his back against the wall of the pit and stroked his cheek. The side of his face which had been burned by the gun explosion was covered with a stubble of new hair. As he stroked it, he made a little rasping sound.

In his long service with the Indian army, he had seen many wounded men, and he knew that doctors could save desperately injured men. But there was no doctor in Chandwari.

In the light of the lamp at Kalu's feet, he looked at the boy's face. Kalu's large, dark eyes were pleading for help, and the old Sikh decided he must try.

"I am no doctor, Kalu," he said quietly, "but I have seen broken legs mended. I am willing to try to mend this cow's leg, but don't blame me if I fail."

"What do we do?" Kalu asked anxiously.

"We put the broken ends together and hold them together by means of what doctors call splints. These are pieces of flat wood which are held against the broken leg by bandages. If the broken parts can be kept together for a few weeks, the leg mends. We'll need rags for bandages and two flat pieces of wood. One of us will have to go to the village for those, and I think I had better go. I know exactly what is needed. Give me a hand out of here. Get on top and I'll give you the lamp. Then you can help me up."

He heaved Kalu upward, then handed him the lamp. Kalu looked round and could see no farther than the little area lit by the light of the lamp. Beyond that, everything seemed pitch black.

"Give me a hand," Havildar Singh said, reaching up. After a brief scramble he lay panting on the pit top. "I'm not as nimble as I used to be," he puffed. "At one time I could have leaped out of that pit with a rifle in my hand and thought . . ." He stopped, for Kalu had given a frightened gasp.

"What's the . . . ?" Havildar Singh asked.

"Over there," Kalu whispered, and pointed.

In silence they both stared into the night which was so deathly quiet that Kalu could hear the pounding of his heart.

"Where?" the old Sikh asked, squinting his eyes. "I can't . . . aaaah!" The quick gasp came as he saw a slight movement. In the lamplight he

could see a striped form and two eyes which shone
luminous. They were like little green moons, blotted
out when the tiger blinked, but reappearing again
almost at once.

"Don't move," Havildar Singh cautioned in a
low whisper. "He may not have seen us."

Kalu was half squatting, with all his weight on his right leg. For perhaps a minute tiger and humans stared at each other, neither moving nor making a sound. Then Kalu's right leg began to cramp. As he moved the cramped muscle could not bear the weight, and Kalu almost toppled over into the pit.

A menacing growl rose from the tiger. The striped and whiskered head moved closer to the ground. The beast was crouching to get into a better position for a leap.

Havildar Singh stretched out both hands—one to steady Kalu, the other to grab the lamp. As he moved, the tiger moved. It leaped toward them, and in the lamplight it was a terrifying sight. The eyes blazed bright green while its wide-open jaws revealed the fearsome teeth.

Havildar Singh started to rise, gripping Kalu with his left hand, swinging the lamp off the ground with his right. His strength in that moment of crisis was amazing. With one swift movement he not only jerked Kalu half to his feet but managed to drag him back a yard. At the same time he swung the lamp in a semicircle in front of him, left and right, right and left—a threat to the tiger if it came too near. He let out screech after screech in the hope that he would startle the tiger into turning tail and making for safety.

Neither the lamp nor the old man's screeches had any effect. The tiger covered eighteen feet in its first spring. Its second spring would take it onto either the Sikh or Kalu, whichever one had not descended into the pit.

In the yellow lamplight the tiger was a terrifying spectacle. Its jaws were wide, its teeth glinting. Its mighty forepaws were wide stretched, ready to deal a killing blow. As it completed its leap, the four paws came together to give that balance necessary for a second leap. It sank down, its weight cushioned by the padded paws, but instead of rising again, the tiger shattered the silence with a howl of agony. Its eyes, which had been shining green, closed; and the killer of a moment before squirmed and lost its balance as it almost fell on its nose.

Havildar Singh bundled Kalu over the rim of the pit and would have followed him immediately had there not been a wail of anguish from the boy and a loud bellow from the cow. Kalu had dropped onto the cow's ribs, then across its horns, and fear had brought the shriek from him.

Havildar, waiting for the tiger to pounce on him, held the lamp high. To his amazement the tiger slowly got to its feet, then turned and limped away. It held its right forepaw off the ground. The injury in that forepaw had been forgotten in the excitement of the encounter with Kalu and Havildar Singh. Now the pain must have been unbearable, for the tiger was making the night hideous with its moans and howls.

Kalu felt certain that the old Sikh must have injured the tiger. "Will it die?" he asked.

Havildar Singh shook his head. He was concerned about the cow. The roaring of the tiger had frightened her, and now she was trying to stand up. She began bellowing even louder when Kalu hurriedly pressed his weight on her back to hold her down. "Lie down," he ordered.

"Quieten it, Kalu. Quieten it," Havildar Singh pleaded. "Or that striped *shaitan* will come back, and he won't fail a second time."

"Can you find something to tie around its jaws?" Kalu asked.

Havildar Singh took off his army bush jacket. It was a threadbare tunic, still decorated with old brass regimental buttons. With this they managed to muffle the mooing of the cow.

"Sit on her haunches," Kalu said, wiping the sweat from his face. "Cows always get up back legs first, and she'll stop struggling if you sit on her haunches."

The old man and the boy fought to get back their breath. The roaring had stopped, and the silence was more frightening. Now they did not know where the tiger was.

"We'll have to wait until morning," Havildar Singh said.

"But the broken leg?" Kalu queried. "Will it not get worse if it is not tied up properly?"

"I suppose it will." Havildar Singh sighed as he added: "But what can we do? Better for the cow to die than for one of us to be struck down and eaten."

Kalu closed his eyes and shivered at the thought of the cow dying. After a minute he said: "If you'll tell me what I must get, I'll go home and get the rags and the pieces of wood."

"And be killed before you got back," was the quick reply. "No."

"But I've got to do something," Kalu protested. "If the cow dies, we shall be ruined."

Havildar rubbed at his chin, making the bristly side rasp under his fingers. He turned up the lamp and examined the cow's broken leg. "I am no doctor, Kalu," he murmured, "yet I feel sure this is a clean break. If it were splinted, she would walk again."

"Then I shall go for the rags . . ."

"No!" Havildar was emphatic. "What would I say to the people of Chandwari Village if you were killed? Surely there must be some other way."

In the rectangle of sky visible from the pit, the stars shone down like a million lamps. Looking up at them Kalu saw the flimsy gate of old boarding they had erected to hold the noose when they had tried to kill Burra Dhantwallah.

Suddenly he let out a shriek of triumph. "Look up there! Wouldn't that do for splinting the cow's leg?" And without waiting for the old man to agree, he climbed out of the pit.

The coarse string which held the gateway together seemed to creak agonizingly as Kalu fumbled with the knots, his ears straining to catch the least sound from the tiger.

Havildar hugged him when he was back in the pit. They had to break the strips of wood, and each break sounded like a pistol shot. They used strips from Havildar Singh's tunic for bandages, and though the cow lowed mournfully when they took the tunic from around her jaws, she did not struggle when the leg was being splinted.

When Havildar Singh finally sat back on his heels and examined his work by the light of the lamp, he nodded in satisfaction. "I have said I am no doctor," he murmured rather proudly, "but I think if we can keep those splints on, then this cow will live for years. She may limp a little, but that will not worry her."

Kalu was so relieved that he lay back and within minutes had dozed off to sleep. Nor did he waken until the birds known as whistling schoolboys were flying overhead on their way to the water to slake their thirst.

Soon after sunrise there came a great hullabaloo. Approaching the pit were a score of villagers led by the headman. Some of the men had spears, but most of them had gourds and metal dishes which they were beating as hard as they could.

Kalu climbed out of the pit, but when he turned to offer a hand to Havildar Singh, the old Sikh shook his head. "No. If the cow is left alone, she may try to stand, and that would undo all the work of splinting. Tell the headman what we have done. With a full day for the task, we should get the cow back to the village long before sundown."

By now the headman and several of the braver villagers were within a few yards of the pit, and as they realized Kalu was talking to the old man, they looked at one another in amazement.

"The gods have looked after you," the headman said. "We heard the tiger roaring. The *shaitan* sounded in such a terrible rage that every door was bolted."

Kalu told the crowd everything and then explained how Havildar Singh had splinted the cow's broken leg. "Mr. Headman, won't you help us get the cow out?" he ended.

"We need ropes and things," the headman said

unhappily, and added: "In any case, whoever heard of a cow being carried to its shed!"

"Mr. Singh knows how to do it," Kalu said eagerly, and he realized at once that he had spoken too soon. The headman turned on him with an angry sneer: "Mr. Singh knows everything! What a pity he isn't the headman of Chandwari Village."

From the pit came a soothing comment from the old Sikh. "You must forgive the boy, Mr. Headman. He is eager to save the life of this cow. I will do what I can to help, but of course everything is in your hands."

The headman grunted and began to look around as if trying to decide what was the best thing to do. An older man made a suggestion, but before anyone could reply, a sound was heard which made the villagers look toward the bushes a mere thirty feet away.

"What was that?" the headman asked, and got his answer immediately. Out into the open, looking magnificent in the morning sun, stepped a full-grown tiger.

A goat for the tiger

The crowd stared in terror at the striped beast.
If they had used their metal plates and gourds,
banging them as hard as they could, chances are
the tiger would have slipped back into the bushes.
Instead, two of the men turned and ran. In an
instant the others followed. The panic spread.

Kalu was as filled with terror as the rest. He too
ran and soon overtook the headman, slowing down
only when he was about a hundred yards from the
village. Startled women and children crowded into
the narrow street as the men came panting into
view. The pi-dogs yapped and snarled, but kept out
of the way.

The headman was last, and having looked over
his shoulder once or twice and not caught sight of
the tiger, he slowed down to a jog-trot. By this time

the story was being told of the gigantic tiger which had come so close.

Kalu went straight to the village well. Throughout the night he had grown increasingly thirsty. Now he drank until beads of perspiration covered his body. He sluiced water over himself and felt better. Going to the house he prepared some food and ate. It gave him time to think; his thoughts were on Mr. Singh and the cow.

"They are both thirsty," he muttered sadly. "If the cow doesn't get water before sunset, she might die. Cows drink a lot of water."

Kalu decided to go to the headman and ask for help. A group of men were talking outside the headman's house, but they stopped as Kalu drew near and turned to stare at him.

As Kalu pleaded with the headman and the village elders to help him rescue Mr. Singh and the cow, others gathered to listen. Some of the women began to protest. Why should a husband risk his life and face a hungry tiger? As for Mr. Singh, he was not even one of the village. He was an outsider.

"But if all the men came with spears and made a great noise," Kalu pleaded, "the tiger would run away."

"I'll see who is willing to help," the headman

finally agreed. Facing the crowd, he asked volunteers to raise their hands.

A few of the younger men raised their hands and then looked uneasily around. When they saw that most of the men were not volunteering, the hands went down. The headman did not speak, but turned to Kalu and shook his head gravely.

It was then that one of the oldest men in the village spoke up. In his thin, squeaky voice he said: "I remember when I was a young man, the British were here. They loved shooting tigers, and they had their own way of doing it. I went out with them many a time . . . and helped them skin the *shaitans* afterward."

"Does that help the boy?" the headman asked sarcastically. "The British have gone from our land for many years. They are not here now to shoot tigers."

"I know, but they had a way which young Kalu might try," the old man squeaked back. "They would buy an old cow, or even a goat. They tied the animal under a tree at night, and they sat up on a *machan* (platform built in the tree). The cow or the goat got lonely, began to cry out, and along came the tiger. Then the white man would shoot it."

"And so?" the headman snapped impatiently. "All we want is a white man with a rifle, and someone to give a goat or a cow. Go home, old man, you live in the dreams of long ago."

"But I don't!" the white-bearded villager protested. "I am trying to tell you how you can rescue Havildar Singh and the cow. Take a goat to the pit. The tiger will kill it, drag it away, and eat it. Tigers only kill when they are hungry. Once it has eaten, it will be satisfied."

"A good idea," a young married woman said angrily. "All we need is someone mad enough to take the goat to the tiger. Or do you think it will walk there alone and let itself be killed? It is a silly idea. *My* husband shall not risk his life like that."

Kalu looked anxiously at the headman, hoping that he would not think the idea foolish. The headman patted Kalu on the shoulders and said sadly: "I'm sorry, Kalu, but if the young men will not volunteer, how can you expect older men to risk their lives?"

As Kalu walked back toward the house, he heard the urgent voice of an older woman: "You should not allow a young boy to face a tiger alone, Headman. It is a wrong thing. He will die."

"If he does, it will bring shame on the village,"

another woman said. "Stop him before it is too late."

"How can I stop him, save by locking him up!" the headman snarled.

Kalu went home and filled a large goatskin waterbag to the brim. He made some chapattis, and as he wrapped them in a clean rag, the woman from the next house came in.

She tried to persuade Kalu not to take a goat to the tiger. "You will surely be killed and eaten," she insisted. "I heard you say that the tiger is lame in one forepaw. It must be the same tiger we have heard calling through the past week. If a tiger is lame, then it cannot hunt; so this tiger will be starving. A starving tiger will even attack humans."

"I am taking our black goat," Kalu said. "The tiger will eat her."

"But you will have to take the goat right to the spot," the woman pointed out. "Don't do it, Kalu. Think of your poor mother and father. If you are killed, after the accident to your father, they will be broken-hearted. Don't do it."

"I must try to rescue Mr. Singh and the cow," he said quietly.

When he had packed all he was taking, some of the village boys helped him tie up the black nanny.

Along with the other goats, the black one had been bleating away since sunrise, asking to be let out. The little flock had not been given water and were also hungry.

Kalu had chosen the black nanny for several reasons. She was the oldest of their goats, and she was also the most bad-tempered. She bullied the others and more than once had butted Kalu for no reason at all.

The boys kept the other goats in, promising to give them water when Kalu had led the black nanny away.

By the time he was ready, Kalu felt even more nervous when he saw all the villagers gathered to see him start. Silent groups of men, women, and even children stood about watching. The only sounds were those made by household pigs rootling among the garbage heaps, and the low clucking of hens.

Kalu slung the little satchel containing food over his shoulder. One of the women helped him lift the goatskin waterbag onto his head. The black nanny was impatiently tugging at the long rope which held her in check. Kalu picked up his father's spear, then loosened the nanny's rope.

As he did so, the headman called: "Wait, Kalu.

No man shall ever say that I allowed a neighbor's
son to face a tiger alone. Wife, get me my spear. I
shall go with the boy."

Some of the younger men now turned and ran
to fetch their spears—and soon there was a little
procession of armed men following Kalu.

The black goat strained at the rope, bleating

hungrily. Once she realized they were going on the way to the best pasture—the patch of spring-fed ground which grew lush grass even in the driest summer—she bleated joyfully and dragged even harder at her rope.

Kalu looked back once and saw the little groups of villagers still staring after the procession. He had the feeling that the people were sure they would never again see him alive. The fact that a dozen armed men followed only yards behind gave him the courage to go on.

Soon they reached the beginning of the cultivated land. A thick thorn hedge grew on his left, while on his right the ground sloped gently upward. The slope was dotted with bushes which grew thicker the farther he went along.

A light breeze was blowing, and since it came from behind him, it would blow the scent of the goat ahead. If the tiger was still waiting, it would get the scent of the goat long before the goat caught the tiger's scent.

When they reached his father's land, he could see the pit, but there was no sign of life. The cow was not lowing, and that made his heart sink. Was it dead?

He looked anxiously over his shoulder and saw to his alarm that the village men were now at least twenty yards behind him.

From the moment they left the village, the black nanny had strained on the rope, almost as if she was afraid all the best grass would be eaten before she got to the grazing patch. As she drew level with the pit, she was still tugging, but the rope went slack as she stopped and Kalu walked on a pace. Then he stopped, and his mouth went bone dry, for just ahead a big tiger had stepped out from the bushes.

The goat stood as if paralyzed, making no sound or movement. Her yellow eyes were fixed on the tiger who was glaring at her through eyes slitted against the sunshine. It was a large tiger but so thin that its coat hung loosely on its flanks.

Kalu released the rope. He knew what he had to do. While the tiger was killing the goat, he must dash for the pit, yell a warning to Mr. Singh, then heave the goatskin waterbag ahead of him before he dropped down beside the old Sikh.

To reach the pit, however, he had to get much closer to the tiger. He had heard men in the village talk about meeting tigers, and they all gave the same advice: remain completely still. To run was fatal, for any hunter will chase that which runs away.

In the seconds that followed, there was no sound or movement from the goat. The tiger was moving, but so slowly. It was sinking down toward the ground, preparing for a leap. Then from behind Kalu came an agonized yell from the headman: "Run back, Kalu! Drop your waterbag and run!"

The shout broke the spell which seemed to have petrified the goat. Stamping with one tiny hoof, she gave a defiant bleat and then tossed her horned head as if daring the tiger to come near. Kalu winced. He had a feeling that the bleat would spur the tiger into action, and he was right.

Swiftly and smoothly the great striped head sank nearer the ground; then the powerful hindquarters swept the tiger off the ground.

The awkward goat

The tiger came out like a silent juggernaut—eyes blazing, mouth open, and left forepaw swinging. The goat should have died within seconds, but she did not.

From the time she was a young kid, the black one of the flock had been awkward and bad-tempered. She was always doing the unexpected. Now, when the tiger leaped, she did not try to escape. She sank back on her haunches for a split second, and as the tiger swept through the air toward her, she stamped her hoofs on the sun-baked earth and then shot forward to meet the attack.

Down came the tiger's forepaw in a blow that was meant to smash the goat's skull or break the neck. But the black nanny, who had moved forward too swiftly, was under the tiger as the paw came down. And as her horned head went up, it raked the tiger's underparts. This threw her attacker off balance, and as the tiger dropped on all fours, it let out a howl of pain and rage. The weight on the injured forepaw had been agonizing.

Kalu was already near the pit when the tiger hit the ground. Its mighty leap had sent it stumbling on perilously close to the boy.

"Look out, Mr. Singh!" Kalu screamed, and lowering his head tipped the goatskin waterbag toward the pit edge. Then he leaped forward, aiming for the safety of the six-foot-deep hole.

From the pit came a mournful bellow, telling Kalu that the injured cow was still alive. Havildar Singh was also shouting. It was more of a croak, for the old man was suffering badly from thirst.

Kalu sat down on the haunches of the cow, for she was struggling wildly to rise. She had been lying still for an hour or more, suffering from thirst; but now the roar of the tiger had terrified her.

"Lie still, you old fool," Havildar Singh croaked. "Have I torn up my tunic for bandages so that you can undo my good work!" Strangely, the cow stopped struggling.

Havildar Singh then grabbed the goatskin

waterbag and hurriedly untied the neck. He looked gratefully at Kalu. "How beautiful is water when you are as thirsty as I am."

While the old man quenched his thirst, the goat was fighting for its life. Kalu's father had often said that their black nanny had a devil between her horns. Now she was demonstrating this. After throwing the tiger off balance, she spun around as nimbly as a ballet dancer; and as the tiger regained its balance, the goat struck again. She charged in silence, her hoofs kicking up puffs of yellow dust.

Catching the tiger in the ribs just as it was beginning to turn, she bowled it over. The nanny's hard head was like a battering ram, and the tiger was not expecting a second attack. With a blood-curdling roar, the tiger lurched to its feet, but by this time the goat was retreating. As if she knew she could not hope to surprise the tiger a third time, she made for a patch of prickly bushes.

She charged into a part of the bushes where the thorns were thinnest. Even so, she left patches of her silky black hair on the savagely strong thorns. Near the center of the bush, where the branches hung down like ribs of an umbrella, she managed to turn. She faced the way she had entered the bush, and her eyes were like balls of golden fire as she waited for the tiger.

Half crazed with pain and rage, the tiger limped after her. He had not eaten for more than a week and was hungry enough to follow food anywhere. He plunged blindly into the opening where he had seen the black goat disappear.

Seconds later, spitting and snarling and leaving

little tufts of yellow and black fur on a circle of thorns, the tiger backed out of the bushes. He was howling even more furiously. The thorns, which were as hard and straight as oversized needles, had stabbed him in a score of places, and two thorns had driven into his tenderest spot, the nose. To add to his fury, the nanny goat was bleating defiance, almost daring the tiger to try again. She too had deep scratches on her flanks from which drops of blood were oozing.

From the depths of the pit, Kalu and Havildar Singh heard the roars and howls of pain from the tiger. But the black nanny was also bleating away.

"The goat does not sound as if she's dying," said Kalu.

"Forget the goat," Havildar Singh said. "If we don't give this cow some water, she'll die. Hold her head up, and I'll see if I can pour water down her throat."

The cow could smell the water and was bellowing madly and twisting her neck in an effort to get near the goatskin waterbag. If Havildar Singh had not been sitting firmly on her hindquarters, she would have risen and done further damage to her splinted leg.

The moment the waterbag was at the cow's

mouth, her struggles ceased. She drank and drank until Havildar Singh finally dragged the bag away. "We can't let her drink the lot," he said, knotting the string about the bag top. "There's no knowing how long we may be in this pit."

Releasing the cow's head, Kalu looked at the footholds which the Sikh had gouged in one of the walls. Using these, the old man had been able to climb up and look over the rim of the pit.

"You can look now," Havildar Singh said, nodding. "But don't get up too high. The tiger does not sound too pleased."

Quietly Kalu dragged himself high enough to look over the rim. Even so, the tiger must have detected something, for he was looking in the direction of the pit. Seconds later he came limping over.

Hastily Havildar Singh wrapped a strip of cloth from his bush jacket around the cow's jaws to stop it from bawling. Neither Kalu nor the old Sikh had ever seen a tiger at such close range. Although the pit was six feet deep, it seemed far too shallow for safety. The big striped beast poked its head over the edge of the pit. He was so close that the tips of the thorns in his nose were visible.

Glaring down at them, the tiger snarled throatily. It moved forward a few inches and then

stretched its left paw down into the pit like a cat pawing in a goldfish bowl.

The cow began to struggle, and Kalu slithered across its bony hindquarters to prevent it from rising. Havildar Singh stroked the wet neck, speaking soothingly to it.

As the tiger inched a little nearer the pit top, its weight descended on the injured right paw. The pain caused the glaring yellow eyes to close, and the mouth opened wide. With a moan of anguish the tiger eased up onto its left paw, its gnawing hunger forgotten. Then it drew back, and its moaning grew less as it moved further away from the pit.

"Allah be praised," Havildar Singh murmured, wiping great beads of sweat from his face. "I thought we were at the end."

Several minutes passed before Kalu or the old Sikh dared move. They secured the strip of cloth around the cow's jaws once more.

"If she starts to bellow again, it could mean the finish," Havildar Singh warned. "I don't know how long it is since that striped *shaitan* had food, but its skin hangs like an old dress. Its injured leg has prevented it from hunting, and a starving tiger will do anything for food. We've got to keep quiet."

They lay in the pit, making no movement, making no sound. Noon came, and still they dared not risk leaving their hideout. The heat increased until the pit was like a furnace. The sun shone straight into it, and the dried earth walls acted like reflectors. They threw the heat back onto man, boy, and cow.

In the shade of a bush only a dozen yards from the pit, the tiger was squatting. It was watching the thorn bush into which the goat had retreated.

Just after noon, when Kalu was unable to stand the thirst any longer, Havildar Singh agreed that they should have a drink and give the cow more water. She was gasping and breathing very shallowly. Kalu drank after the cow had been given a pint or so and was shocked when the old Sikh pushed the goatskin waterbag away. Throughout the morning he had been sucking a pebble. "Suck a pebble, Kalu," he urged. "It's a help when you are thirsty."

Slowly the afternoon began to pass. Kalu kept thinking of the cool, sparkling water of the village well from which people drew up bucketsful. Twice he was ready to climb out of the pit and slip down to the village. Each time Havildar Singh glared at him and shook his head.

As the sun set and the sky above the pit turned deep blue, Havildar Singh slumped forward.

Anxiously Kalu heaved him back to a sitting position, and the old Sikh opened his eyes. He shook his head as if trying to drive away the mists clouding his brain. "I am all right," he muttered, but his voice was thick.

"I am going for water," Kalu said firmly. "I am not going to let you die."

"Not yet," Havildar Singh pleaded. "That *shaitan* of a tiger must be as thirsty as we are. He will go for water. That will be the time."

Kalu sat down again, while overhead the sky darkened. Quickly the sunset faded into night. Havildar Singh seemed to have fallen asleep, and Kalu's anxiety increased. At last he could wait no longer.

Placing a hand on Havildar Singh's shoulder, he shook the old man gently. "Mr. Singh, I am going for water."

"There will be a moon, and the tiger will see you," Havildar Singh murmured. "Wait, for he may go to drink."

Kalu did not argue. Using the niches cut into the pit wall, he got up high enough to look out. The light in the west was no more than a thin red line on the far horizon. To the east there was a growing patch of silver on the hilltops. The moon was rising.

The tiger was still in sight, but now he was limping away from the bush. Kalu waited eagerly. He felt sure the tiger would turn westward and move toward the patch of wet ground where the cattle grazed. There it could drink. Instead, the tiger turned in the direction of the village.

Dropping back into the pit, Kalu grabbed the empty goatskin bag. "I'm going down to the spring where the cattle graze," he said. "The tiger has gone off, but toward the village."

"Be careful," Havildar Singh croaked, but he still seemed in a daze.

Scrambling out of the pit, Kalu headed for the marshy spot where the cattle grazed. The night was very quiet, and the patter of his bare feet on the hard ground seemed to bring a ghostly echo from the bushes on the higher ground. Fear kept him going.

He splashed through the marshy fringe of land surrounding the spring, drank until he could drink no more, then snatched up the goatskin bag which he had plunged deep into the little pool. It was only a third full, but he was afraid to wait for it to fill.

With the wet bag flopping on his head, he raced back the way he had come, and the moonlight seemed almost as bright as day. The sky was cloudless, and the moon, a shining silver.

Somewhere an owl hooted, but he did not hear it. He could hear only the pulsing thud at his temples and the flip-flap-flip of the waterbag on his head. He panted up the slope which led to the pit and was no more than six yards from it when the tiger stepped out to meet him.

Kalu stopped so suddenly that the goatskin waterbag slipped off his head and flopped at his feet. The tiger snarled softly at the sound and stopped, its injured paw raised. Kalu could see the pit, a rectangle of black showing clearly in the moonlight. He looked at the tiger, and he knew he could not reach the pit.

"I said I would
kill the boar"

Like a rabbit which crouches motionless, hypnotized by a stoat or a weasel, Kalu stood and stared at the tiger. His mind had stopped working. The tiger's tail was twitching from side to side. It was gathering itself for a spring.

Suddenly its tail stopped twitching, and the tiger lifted itself erect. It looked back toward the moonlit hillside dotted with hundreds of bushes. Like someone in a dream, Kalu heard the sound which had distracted the tiger. There came a pattering and a vague chorus of low grunts and squeaks.

The tiger moved to one side and seemed to vanish into the shadows of a big bush. Within seconds there was a loud grunt, and Burra Dhant-wallah raced down almost to the rim of the pit. His family was with him: the old sow, the half-grown boars and sows, and the squeaking piglets.

As swiftly as it had vanished, the tiger reappeared from the shadows and growled. The grunting stopped, and even the squeaking of the piglets died away. There was a quick shuffling of feet, and the family of wild pigs turned to face their worst enemy.

The tiger stepped forward, teeth bared in a silent snarl. Burra Dhantwallah grunted a reply and brushed his way through his family until he faced the tiger. The rest of the pigs began to edge away.

Sinking down, the tiger snarled again, a snarl that was intended to panic the young pigs and make them scatter. Then he would snatch one.

Burra Dhantwallah grunted, and the agitated piglets and young sows stood their ground. Growing impatient, the tiger stalked forward, limping heavily. The old sow grunted in alarm. At once the piglets squealed and began to scatter, fleeing for safety. The tiger turned, meaning to grab one, and at that moment Burra Dhantwallah charged. It was not unexpected, and the tiger sank back on its haunches and flailed at the boar with its strong left paw. Burra Dhantwallah tried to swing away from the bone-crushing blow, but he was rolled over.

The tiger pounced, seeking a grip on the throat. Three or four hundred pounds of boar was far better than a small piglet. But the tiger missed his aim, and his teeth merely nipped at the boar's shoulder. An instant later Burra Dhantwallah rose, and the tiger was flung to one side.

It rolled over. Speedily it rose to its feet again. For a split second Kalu, who crouched by the thorn hedge only a few yards away, was sure the glittering eyes were on him.

At that moment Burra Dhantwallah, his shoulder streaming blood, came in, his tusks glinting in the moonlight. The peace of the night was shattered in an instant. Snarls and screeches from the tiger mingled with the savage grunts of Burra Dhantwallah. Once the tiger drew back, as if willing to let the boar get away.

Burra Dhantwallah, raked from shoulder to tail by the tiger's savage claws, seemed to be rocking on his short legs. Then he charged. For two minutes tiger and boar seemed to be a tangle of legs and heads, tusks gouging, claws lacerating.

The two animals rolled apart, and the tiger raised its head for a moment and snarled; then the head sank back to the ground. The long, striped form relaxed as if the tiger had drifted off to sleep.

Burra Dhantwallah had also rolled over, but he rose
to his feet.

He was groggy. He lurched forward a pace, as
if to make sure the tiger really was dead; but the
effort was too much. His short, sturdy legs gave
way, and he flopped to the ground, his flanks heaving.

Kalu, who had been trapped in the midst of the battle, got to his feet. He picked up the goatskin waterbag, and water splashed onto his feet. The terror of the past minutes had been so great that Kalu was not aware he was losing the water until he reached the pit and almost fell down alongside Havildar Singh and the moaning cow.

"What's happened?" Havildar Singh asked. Feeling the waterbag, he lifted it to his lips, but got hardly enough to wet his parched throat. "Where's the water?"

Kalu stared at him for a moment. He was still shocked from the battle he had witnessed; but when the old man asked again for water, Kalu snatched up the goatskin bag, saying: "I'll go back to the spring."

"Go to the village," Havildar Singh ordered. "Tell them. If they know the tiger is dead, they'll come. They'll want a share of the pork, and they'll get this dying cow out of the pit. Hurry, boy. And bring a spear back with you," he added. "Boars don't die easily. With a spear you can finish Burra Dhantwallah for certain."

Kalu scrambled out of the pit. He stood for a moment looking at the tiger. It was lying motionless. The boar was breathing; and as Kalu drew closer, the head lifted, the eyes opened, and Burra Dhantwallah grunted a warning.

"Wait," Kalu shouted. "You shall not grunt when I come back. I will bring a spear. You'll ruin no more of my father's crops."

At Kalu's shout there came an anxious bleating. Moments later the black nanny broke free from the bushes and came racing after him.

There was great excitement in the village when Kalu arrived with the news. He urged the headman to get the younger men to come along with ropes to rescue the cow.

"I'll go back at once," Kalu told the gathering crowd of men, women, and children. "But I need a spear and a lamp. And I'll take water for Mr. Singh and the cow."

Kalu was lowering the bag of water to Havildar Singh when the first of the villagers arrived.

"Where is the boar?" they asked, kneeling at the edge of the pit. "You said the boar is dead, Kalu Lal."

"I said he was dying," Kalu insisted, getting to his feet. "I brought the spear to finish him off. Bring a lamp and I'll show you where he lay. You can still see the blood."

"There would have been pork for everyone," the headman said regretfully.

"There will be a blood trail," one of the men said. "We could follow him up the hill."

"Do you want to join Kunwar Lal in the hospital?" the headman asked sourly. "Only a fool would hunt a wounded boar at night."

"He was badly injured," Kalu said. "Maybe he will have died before sunrise."

"There will be no free pork for the people of Chandwari," one man said grimly. "If the boar dies, either vultures or jackals will have him before any Chandwari man discovers him."

Nothing more was said, and the men got busy rescuing the cow from the pit. Soon after midnight the cow was installed in a small open-ended shed. She could be fed at the front, and her broken leg could be attended to from the other end. Bands of cloth from one side of the shed to the other had been fastened under her so that she could not put any weight on her legs. She seemed content enough when they left her, for she had drank all the water she wanted and had been given a good feed. In a few weeks she could be taken out of the shed, for her leg would have mended.

Next morning Kalu awakened when Havildar Singh came in with a cup of tea and some chapattis.

Suddenly the old Sikh asked: "How far away from you was Burra Dhantwallah when he got up last night and walked away?"

For a moment Kalu said nothing. He chewed, swallowed the piece of chapatti, and then asked: "You know?"

The old man smiled. "I heard you come back from the village, and I wondered why you were so long lowering the water to me. Were you doing something to the old boar?"

"You will think me a fool, Mr. Singh," Kalu said very quietly. "I brought a spear from the village, for I meant to kill the boar. It was only when I put the lamp near him and raised the spear that he looked up at me. He knew what I meant to do, and he tried to get to his feet. He was badly hurt, but he was not going to die without a fight."

"But you didn't kill him," Havildar Singh said.

"No." Kalu shook his head. "I suddenly remembered that if he had not fought the tiger, I might have been dead . . . and you . . . and the cow. . . ."

"So you spared his life?"

"I gave him a drink," Kalu said. "Then I prodded him with the butt end of the spear until he got up and crawled around the back of the bushes."

Havildar Singh smiled. "I guessed you had done something. I saw him this morning, and I could have killed him; but soldiers do not kill wounded enemies. That is one of the rules of warfare. I gave him water, and I could see strength flowing back into him. He finally got up, and the last I saw of him he was walking slowly up the hill. I don't think he'll die—and I don't think the pigs will trouble us again."

Havildar Singh was right. Some days later he and Kalu made their way up the hill through the scattered bushes to the stony top where Burra Dhantwallah and his family had spent the daytime hours. The pigs were not there. Nor was there any sign of bones to suggest that the old boar had died and his carcass picked clean by the vultures.

When Kalu's father and mother returned to Chandwari a few weeks later, it was to find the crops in their field growing well. The headman welcomed Kunwar Lal home and said: "There is a tale to tell, O man who should be proud of his son.

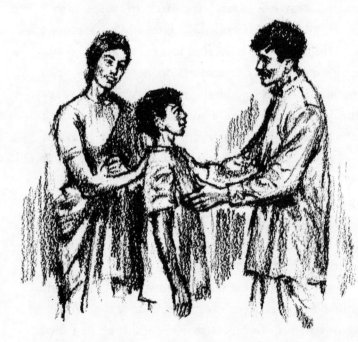

You are father to a boy who did what none of us could do—he kept the promise he made to drive away the pigs. They have gone, and it was Kalu who drove them away. The story of Kalu and the wild boar will be told many times before it is forgotten."